Clarion Books
a Houghton Mifflin Company imprint
215 Park Avenue South, New York, NY 10003
Text and illustrations copyright © 1996 by Jan Ormerod

First published in the United Kingdom 1995 by The Bodley Head
Children's Books, Random House, 20 Vauxhall Bridge Road,
London SW1V 2SA.

Printed in Hong Kong

Library of Congress Cataloging-in-Publication Data

Ormerod, Jan.
Ms. MacDonald has a class / [author and illustrator] Jan
Ormerod.
p.   cm.
"First published in the United Kingdom by The Bodley
Head Children's Books, Random House"—T.p. verso.
Includes musical notation for Old MacDonald's Farm.
Summary: After visiting the farm, the children in Ms.
MacDonald's class learn to move and look and sound very
different while preparing to present the performance of a
lifetime.
ISBN 0-395-77611-2
[1. Theater—Fiction. 2. Schools—Fiction. 3. Stories
in rhyme.]   I. Title.
PZ8. 3. 0718Ms   1996
[E]—dc20
                                        95-38192
                                           CIP
                                           AC

10 9 8 7 6 5 4 3 2 1

Jan Ormerod

Ms. MacDonald
Has a Class

Clarion Books
New York

Ms. MacDonald has a class, E-I-E-I-O,
She takes her class down to the farm, E-I-E-I-O,

With a pigpen here and a hay bale there,
Here a bucket, "Where's your boots?" everywhere a chick chick,

Ms. MacDonald has a class, E-I-E-I-O.

Ms. MacDonald has a class, E-I-E-I-O,
And in that class they make some plans, E-I-E-I-O,

With a "What's this?" here and a "Do what?" there,
Here a chatter, there a natter, everywhere a pitter patter,
Ms. MacDonald has a class, E-I-E-I-O.

Ms. MacDonald has a class, E-I-E-I-O,
And in that class they flip flap flop, E-I-E-I-O,

With a skip trip here and a hop step there,
Here a jump, there a bump, everywhere a boing boing,

A "What's this?" here and a "Do what?" there,
Here a chatter, there a natter, everywhere a pitter patter,
Ms. MacDonald has a class, E-I-E-I-O.

Ms. MacDonald has a class, E-I-E-I-O,
And in that class they sing along, E-I-E-I-O,

With a tra-la here and a tra-la there,
Here a tra, there a la, everywhere a tra-la,

A skip trip here and hop step there,
Here a jump, there a bump, everywhere a boing boing,

A "What's this?" here and a "Do what?" there,
Here a chatter, there a natter, everywhere a pitter patter,
Ms. MacDonald has a class, E-I-E-I-O.

Ms. MacDonald has a class, E-I-E-I-O,
And in that class they make some sounds, E-I-E-I-O,

With a boom boom here and a ting-a-ling there,
Here a boom, there a ting, everywhere a boom-a-ling,

A tra-la here and a tra-la there,
Here a tra, there a la, everywhere a tra-la,

A skip trip here and a hop step there,
Here a jump, there a bump, everywhere a boing boing,

A "What's this?" here and a "Do what?" there,
Here a chatter, there a natter, everywhere a pitter patter,

Ms. MacDonald has a class, E-I-E-I-O.

Ms. MacDonald has a class, E-I-E-I-O,
And in that class they snip and stitch, E-I-E-I-O,

With a snip snip here and a stitch stitch there,
Here a snip, there a stitch, everywhere a snip stitch,

A boom boom here and a ting-a-ling there,
Here a boom, there a ting, everywhere a boom-a-ling,

With a tra-la here and a tra-la there,
Here a tra, there a la, everywhere a tra-la,

A skip trip here and a hop step there,
Here a jump, there a bump, everywhere a boing boing,

A "What's this?" here and a "Do what?" there,
Here a chatter, there a natter, everywhere a pitter patter,
Ms. MacDonald has a class, E-I-E-I-O.

Ms. MacDonald has a class, E-I-E-I-O,
And in that class they paint and glue, E-I-E-I-O,

With a slap slop here and a splish splash there,
Here a slop, there a splash, everywhere a drip drop,

A snip snip here and a stitch stitch there,
Here a snip, there a stitch, everywhere a snip stitch,

A boom boom here and a ting-a-ling there,
Here a boom, there a ting, everywhere a boom-a-ling,

A tra-la here and a tra-la there,
Here a tra, there a la, everywhere a tra-la,

A skip trip here and a hop step there,
Here a jump, there a bump, everywhere a boing boing,

A "What's this?" here and a "Do what?" there,
Here a chatter, there a natter, everywhere a pitter patter,
Ms. MacDonald has a class, E-I-E-I-O.

Ms. MacDonald has a class, E-I-E-I-O,
And in that class they tidy up, E-I-E-I-O,

With the paper here and the scissors there,
Here a lid, there a wipe, everybody wash hands,

A "Yum yum" here and a "Yum yum" there,
Here a "Yum," there a "Yum," everywhere a "Yum yum,"

A "SHHH" here and a "SHHH" there,
Here a "SHHH," there a "SHHH," everywhere a ZZZ-ZZZ,
Ms. MacDonald has a class, E-I-E-I-O.

Ms. MacDonald has a class, E-I-E-I-O,
And in that class they're almost there, E-I-E-I-O,

With a "One chair here?" and a "Two chairs there?"
Here a plink, there a plonk, everywhere a "Watch out!"

A fluffy tail here and a spotty face there,
Here a "Ready," there a "Steady," everywhere a "Let's Go!"

A moo moo here and a moo moo there,
Here a brmm, there a brmm, everywhere a cheep cheep,

A scarecrow here and a crow crow there,
Here a cluck, there a squawk, everywhere a cockle-doodle,

A woof woof here and a baa baa there,
Here a baa, there a baa, everywhere a baa baa,

An oink oink here and an oink oink there,
Here a hop, there a waddle, everywhere a quack quack,

A gobble gobble here and a gobble gobble there,

Here a nip, there a nip, everywhere a run run...

Ms. MacDonald has a class, E-I-E-I-O.

Ms. MacDonald has a class, E-I-E-I-O,
And in that class they take a bow, E-I-E-I-O,
With a clap clap here and a clap clap there,
Here a clap, there a clap, everywhere a "Hooray!"

Ms. MacDonald has a class, E-I-E-I-O.